Dear Parents:

Congratulations! Your child is taking the first steps on an exciting journey. The destination? Independent reading!

STEP INTO READING® will help your child get there. The program offers five steps to reading success. Each step includes fun stories and colorful art or photographs. In addition to original fiction and books with favorite characters, there are Step into Reading Non-Fiction Readers, Phonics Readers and Boxed Sets, Sticker Readers, and Comic Readers—a complete literacy program with something to interest every child.

Learning to Read, Step by Step!

Ready to Read   Preschool–Kindergarten
• big type and easy words • rhyme and rhythm • picture clues
For children who know the alphabet and are eager to begin reading.

Reading with Help   Preschool–Grade 1
• basic vocabulary • short sentences • simple stories
For children who recognize familiar words and sound out new words with help.

Reading on Your Own   Grades 1–3
• engaging characters • easy-to-follow plots • popular topics
For children who are ready to read on their own.

Reading Paragraphs   Grades 2–3
• challenging vocabulary • short paragraphs • exciting stories
For newly independent readers who read simple sentences with confidence.

Ready for Chapters   Grades 2–4
• chapters • longer paragraphs • full-color art
For children who want to take the plunge into chapter books but still like colorful pictures.

STEP INTO READING® is designed to give every child a successful reading experience. The grade levels are only guides; children will progress through the steps at their own speed, developing confidence in their reading. The F&P Text Level on the back cover serves as another tool to help you choose the right book for your child.

Remember, a lifetime love of reading starts with a single step!

For my mom

—*J.G.*

Text copyright © 2000 by Julie Glass. Cover art and interior illustrations
copyright © 2000 by Joy Allen. All rights reserved. Published in the United States
by Random House Children's Books, a division of Penguin Random House LLC, New York.

Step into Reading, Random House, and the Random House colophon are registered trademarks
of Penguin Random House LLC.

Visit us on the Web!
StepIntoReading.com
randomhousekids.com

Educators and librarians, for a variety of teaching tools, visit us at
RHTeachersLibrarians.com

Library of Congress Cataloging-in-Publication Data
Glass, Julie.
A dollar for Penny / by Julie Glass ; illustrated by Joy Allen.
    p.   cm. — (Step into reading. A step 2 math reader)
Summary: Penny learns about currency when she sets up a lemonade stand to earn
money for her mother's birthday card.
ISBN 978-0-679-88973-1 (trade) — ISBN 978-0-679-98973-8 (lib. bdg.)
[1. Money—Fiction. 2. Moneymaking projects—Fiction. 3. Birthdays—Fiction.
4. Stories in rhyme.]
I. Allen, Joy, ill. II. Title. III. Series: Step into reading. Step 2 math reader.
PZ8.3.G42635 Do 2003 [E]—dc21 2002014524

Printed in the United States of America   26 25 24 23 22 21

This book has been officially leveled by using the F&P Text Level Gradient™ Leveling
System.

A Dollar for Penny

by Dr. Julie Glass

illustrated by Joy Allen

Random House 🏠 New York

In the shade,

I sell lemonade.

I have pink.

Stop and drink!

My aunt Jenny

pays one penny.

In my bank,
one penny goes CLANK.

The price goes up—

to two cents a cup!

Uncle Pete buys two.

Four cents is now due.

In my bank,
the pennies go CLANK!
The price goes up—
to five cents a cup!

Here are my cousins,
Kate and Lou.

They both want lemonade.

Woo-hoo!

Two nickels go CLANK

into my bank.

I have some lunch.

Munch, munch, munch.

For me,
the lemonade is free!

The price goes up—
to ten cents a cup!

Grandma Grime
pays a dime—

into my bank—
clink, clink, CLANK!

The price goes up—

to twenty-five cents a cup!

My sister Lee
gets one cup free!

My brother Sam
plays in a band.
He wants one cup.
He pays up.

In my bank,
one quarter goes
CLANK!

The price goes up—
to fifty cents a cup!
My dad buys one.
Selling lemonade is fun!

Lemonade
50¢

CLANK, clink, CLANK!
Two more quarters
in my bank.

Time to count
the total amount.

= 75¢

= 10¢

= 10¢

= 5¢

"Wow!" I holler.
"One hundred cents
is one dollar!"

I run to the store.

I look in the rack.

The card that I want

is way in the back.

It is red and green
and pink and blue.

Inside it says:

Happy Birthday, Mom.

I love you!

5 pennies   1 nickel

2 nickels   1 dime

2 dimes, 1 nickel   1 quarter

4 quarters   1 dollar